By the Numbers
A Ninjas origin story

Dawn Blair

MORNING SKY STUDIOS

Ninjas: By the Numbers

Copyright © 2017 Dawn Blair

Cover by © Dvmsimages | Dreamstime.com

ISBN: 978-0-9985441-2-0

Morning Sky Studios
P.O. Box 5422
Twin Falls, ID 83301

Visit us online at **www.morningskystudios.com**

Books by Dawn Blair:

Sacred Knight:

The Three Books
Manifest the Magic
To Birth a Destiny
History of a Dead Man
   (companion novella)

The Loki Adventures:

1-800-Mischief
For Sale, Call Loki
For A Good Time, Call Loki
For More Information, Call Loki
For More Mischief, Call Loki

Other stories and novellas

Fractured Echo
The Last Ant
The Doorway Prince

The Write Edit

Sign up for Dawn's newsletter at:

dawnblair.wordpress.com

Ninjas: By the Numbers

When the homeless man had touched her hand, Amanda felt something go through her. She still couldn't identify what it had been, but she knew the significance it held. It made her feel important, as if life held more promise and adventure than she currently experienced. The last few years had seemed like her life had been placed on pause but she couldn't determine if she'd know when her future would ever begin.

That moment of the homeless man's contact held her thoughts as Amanda now stared at the sheet of paper her employer handed to her. It took her a moment to get out of her head to look at exactly what it was that she'd been given. The list of questions on it wanted her goals for the next year. Did he really expect her to answer this? She wanted to look up at her boss, Terry, and ask if this was serious. Instead, she looked up at Terry's soft blue eyes and tried to give him a smile as she said, "Thank you." She felt so damned by her own words.

"I'd like that back as soon as possible," he responded before he turned back toward his office.

"Oh, I'll give it back," she muttered to the paper, her lips moving just enough that only light pops sounded from her mouth. How exactly was she to fill this out? She worked at a travel agency, for Sam's sake! How was she supposed to have goals? She made vacation plans for other people. Her job barely required her to know how to use the phone and computer. Anyone requiring more than a minimum of booking usually went to see Terry for additional advice. He was the one that had to be knowledgeable as well as handling all the marketing for the company. It was his baby. Her goals consisted of show up, help people, and get paid to do it all again tomorrow.

A few weeks ago, it would have been easy to make up something that would please Terry. Then a black-winged angel and a homeless man had set her life back on a new course. So the men hadn't exactly been an angel or homeless, but they had changed her life. She had access to powers she'd long denied and a growing confidence in using her abilities.

Terry had only noticed the addition of her crystal ball to her desk. He thought she was just falling into that "New Age-y" fad that had gripped many people.

Her sugar cookie candle, almost completely expended, burned on her desk now rather than off to the side on the small file cabinet. She'd been debating about getting a replacement candle, but knew the scent evoked the memory of the moment her life had been forever altered. The man and the angel had wanted her to find a boy. She didn't know if they had found him or not. She hoped they had.

Right now, finding that child across the entire span of time for this world seemed easy compared to the list of goal questions sitting before her now.

Her email dinged that she had a new message. She turned to her computer, glad for the distraction that would take her mind off goals for a moment.

She nearly laughed at the email's headline: *Are Your Employees Engaged?*

The article came from a newsletter she frequently liked to read. She read through the teaser, then clicked to open the article.

Actually, she skipped the article and went straight to the infographic.

87% of all employees worked just to pay the bills, the infographic began right after a little cartoon man sat sagging at his desk with his glasses askew.

Yep, Amanda thought, working to pay the bills. A sad state of life, not only for her, but eight-six additional people out of a hundred. Really? Did only thirteen people work, not because they needed the money, but also for enjoyment? Who were those people?

"Terry," she whispered to herself in answer.

She finished scanning through the graphic, finding interest in some of the numbers they were trying to illustrate. Was it really important that 27% of those polled thought computer systems would change in the next five years? In relation to career satisfaction, it seemed irrelevant. As irrelevant as the list of goals that Terry wanted her to compile.

She would fill this out the way she knew Terry wanted her to answer.

If her infographic was up there, she'd say that 9% of employees thought that filling out a goal sheet was important. And those nine people out of every hundred were the most boring and unimaginative people ever. Of course, they had never had their lives changed by an angel and a homeless man.

She also knew that most people weren't happy with the lives they were leading and were too afraid to change. She'd been there, until right now. She stamped her foot on the carpeted floor and turned in her chair as if she were getting ready to stand. She wasn't going to, she wasn't quite that ready, but nearly.

There was something Amanda had always wanted to do, but until she had met her black winged angel and her homeless man she had thought it impossible. But now, maybe, just maybe. She looked at her calendar. Today was Friday the 13th. No, Amanda didn't believe in superstitions. Well, not anymore. Her grandmother had been an oracle too. Amanda watched how her friends had reacted to and then teased her grandmother. That's why Amanda had never wanted to claim her oracle heritage, choosing instead to deny what she was and pretend to be *normal*. She wanted nothing to do with fortune-telling or seeing the future. But she had always known that her grandmother's powers were true. Her grandmother had predicted her future.

It had been on a Friday the 13th when Amanda first admitted that she had seen into the future. She had foreseen her father's accident and tried to explain it to her mother. Her mother didn't want to know. Her mother had denied her oracle heritage as well. So Amanda turned to the one person she knew would believe her: her grandmother.

Her grandmother had set the crystal ball down on the table and then ran her fingers over the tablecloth as though brushing away invisible dust. Then her grandmother had taken out the tarot deck.

"We don't often see deaths, especially of our relatives. Generally, it's only mass deaths that we see," her grandmother explained. "For you to have had a sight with such detail, child, you may be even more powerful than me."

Her grandmother had wondered if Amanda was the oracle spoken of in ancient scrolls. But wasn't that always the way of prophecies? The one to save the world. The one involved in the foretold events. Amanda had more of a desire to be popular than to save the world. Being popular was everything in junior high. Saving the world wasn't something that filled a person's life with friends. In fact, as she'd seen through the countless visits to museums as well as the statues that graced the important buildings in the city, those who tried to change or save the world still ended up dead and barely a notation in history. She wanted to be one of the stars. She wanted to be remembered forever. Fulfilling the oracle's prophecy, didn't make one that.

Amanda didn't remember which tarot cards her grandmother had pulled out, but her grandmother did seem thrilled. She tried to convince Amanda that she was the one, that she would solve the prophecy. Amanda wanted nothing to do with that. She just wanted a date with Bobby.

All that seemed so far in her past and distant now. The last time she'd seen Bobby, he had been balding, had grown a gut that hung way over the waistband of his pants, and had five kids clinging and dancing around him. His wife wasn't much better off. Amanda suspected they both spent a lot of time on the couch watching the television. No grand future there and she had escaped it.

Maybe being an oracle now would be the better option. Those statues that she'd once thought merely footnotes in history, Amanda had grown to love. They had been people with rich histories, people who had done something with their lives, made a difference. Time gave perspective to all things.

And here was today, Friday the 13th. Her day of prophecy.

Amanda got up from her desk and grabbed her purse. The sheet wanting her goals still sat on the desk. She took a pen and scribbled across it, "To save the world." What better goal did you need than that?

"Terry, I'm heading out for lunch." She jangled her keys just to make sure that he was paying attention.

"Have a good one. I'll see you in an hour," he said

Amanda burst for the door. She couldn't wait to get outside, to get started, to begin her new life. She jumped in her car and headed toward the museum.

The trip to the museum only took about five

minutes. How strange it seemed now that her fate awaited her within minutes of where she had been working before her life had changed. Part of her hoped to see the black winged angel and the homeless man there at the museum waiting for her. Unfortunately, there was no one. No one except the museum staff. They didn't charge an admission, so she just walked right on in and began to look around, even though she knew exactly where she needed to go.

Feeling it important to understand her fate, the fate of the world, before she began her mission, she walked through the ancient history.

After leaving the room of prehistory, which could be called speculative theory because no one really knew what had really happened, she entered the room where the first writings began. During this time, crops were planted, trades were made, and people began to barter. The beginning of commercialism. The beginning of civilization.

In the next age, pre-industrialism grew. People were no longer surviving, but thriving. Manufacturing was just beginning.

For as wondrous as this age had been, it quickly fell into disarray as a plague hit, a plague that nearly wiped out the whole planet. There were pictures of the crematoriums, mass factories where the dead were burned. Theory had it that not everyone that had been burned was dead.

One curious thing about the plague was that it all been caused by an object, a simple ceramic jar with a lid. She stood in front of the case now that held the crock that had supposedly released the plague upon the world. No one knew who had caused the plague, and there was some speculation that it had been an offensive military assault in a great battle. But no one even knew who the contestants of the combat were. Some claimed it was the monarchs of the time warring over land, fighting for control of the world. After all, isn't that what all battles are? The jar had also been a source of finding the cure for the plague. But again, how precisely that had happened, no one knew.

Amanda continued to wander. She left this room and strolled into the last where the world was moving into a modern-industrial evolution. Here the crematoriums were being torn down and replaced with factories that manufactured goods for people. Assembly lines were appearing. It gave people jobs and hope. It brought ways of getting better nutrition to the people who had long suffered after the plague. This had marked a whole new way of life for people. Everything that surrounded her and her world today, had begun in this era. But it wasn't perfect either.

Even to this day, people felt like something was missing from their lives. Something magical.

Amanda stood in this room looking around. She felt like the answer was here. But she couldn't see anything other than human invention. There had been no magical hand in this. No inkling that the same power that brought her visions had done anything to help this world in this time.

She closed her eyes, wishing now she would have a vision to know. Nothing came. There was no spark and no electricity to light the way.

As if by their own accord, though she knew it was impossible, her feet began to move beneath her and she walked back into the previous room. She stared at an old picture of the crematoriums there on the wall until she saw it. The homeless man and the black winged angel stood in the background of the picture. They pointed at something that Amanda couldn't quite tell what it was. She inched closer, getting so close that she almost put her nose to the glass. One of the museum staff entered the room. "Did you have family put to rest there?"

Amanda didn't know. The crematoriums records were not that great, so it was hard to tell who exactly had been burned in the crematoriums, let alone which one. She never even thought to look for her own ancestors there. That just felt too morbid. Presumably though, she did. She turned around to tell this to the museum staff, but instead said, "Yes." Now why had she said that? It just felt like the right thing to say.

"We have the ledgers of names," the worker offered, "if you want to look at them."

"I looked them up before," she lied. "But if you have other pictures of the crematorium, I'd be interested in seeing those."

"We do. They're in the archives. Come on, I'll show you."

Amanda followed the staff worker out of this room and downstairs. The employee took a ring of keys and selected one, then unlocked the door in a short hallway at the bottom of the stairs. She twisted the knob and let it swing open. The scent of cleaning supplies rushed out. Since the door probably remained locked most of the time, the room didn't often have a chance to air out. The woman went inside and flipped on the light.

She pulled a couple of big albums off the shelf and set them on the table. "These are gonna be your best bets," she said, flipping open one of the books to a random page then pointed to one of the pictures as if proving to Amanda the truth of her previous statement. As if Amanda had even doubted the clerk.

"Thank you." Amanda pulled the chair out and sat down, more for show than because she actually wanted to sit.

"Let me know if you need anything else," the employee said as she turned to leave the room. Once the door shut and clicked behind her,

Amanda turned to the archive. She went through several pages of the photo album just to make sure that the employee didn't come back immediately. When she didn't, Amanda stood up and began to look around the room. There was a lot more in here than just old books. A couple of glass cases had different relics in them which looked to be quite secure and monitored to preserve the relics. After looking around and finding nothing that drew her interest, Amanda went back to the tables. She needed to find out what her angel and the homeless man had been pointing at. She searched until she found a detailed photograph of the very front of that same building. The only one she wanted, the only one she found, was the most morbid of them all. Outside the front doors, two men were wheeling in a cart full of bodies. One hand hung over the side. It looked to be that of a child nearly in his teen years.

She asked herself what she was doing here, why she felt drawn to be looking through their most morbid time of history. She always hated this part of history class in school. Nor had she ever liked any other. It seemed war and death was all they could teach in high school, as if every educational institution had forgot that history was really about life and the people who had put courage into their lives to change the world.

"It's a wonder we've ever made it this far,"

she muttered quietly to herself.

But in the details of the photograph, she saw it. The numbers on the building read 5402 beside an ornamentation that resembled a star. The decoration had something in the center which she could also see reflected in the photograph but she couldn't quite tell what it was. With all the crematoriums torn down, she wondered what happened to the little star decoration. Had someone taken it and it now resided in their private collection? Had it just got thrown out along with all the other rubble?

The one thing she knew was that this star was a guiding point and would usher her to her destiny. Had it once led the way for her black winged angel and the homeless man?

Marking a place with her finger, she flipped through the book hoping to find another copy of the photograph she'd seen in the main hall. When she didn't find one in this book, she lay her current book open to the page where she was at and began to search through the second book. Here, she found the picture she was after. She could just barely make out one of the points of the star over the shoulder of the man in the foreground of the picture and, yes, her angel was pointing at the star. What had once guided them would guide her now.

She opened the door and signaled for the employee to come help her. As Amanda waited for the clerk to come back in, she looked at the relics in their glass cases again.

Her watch beeped, indicating that she only had ten minutes left before she needed to be back at work. Was it really that time already? She hadn't even had time to pick up some food. Double checking her watch, she found the alarm to be correct. It galled her. She hated bowing to the time constraints of others. For some reason, today it really bothered her. She couldn't wait until she found the key to her freedom.

She turned back to the photograph in the book. Was the key to her freedom right in front of her? The chance that this synchronicity could hold her fate excited her. She fought to be patient, knowing it wasn't time yet. Her new life would take some building. Soon, she painfully reminded herself.

"Five-four-zero-two," she whispered to herself. The numbers added up to eleven, but then if you added the digits together, the answer then became two. What did that number mean to her? A couple, not necessarily romantically involved, could be two friends, perhaps partners on a journey. Two people, like her black-winged angel and the homeless man. They had certainly been the key for her to realize who she was, what she needed to be.

"You are the one of the prophecy," she heard her grandmother's voice whisper in her mind.

Amanda and a prophecy wrapped together

like the double helices of DNA, or the dual snakes which made up caduceus. Two. Opposites, like day and night, light and dark, healthy and sick, love and indifference. Yet, she also knew this was not really opposites, like of only having one and never the other at the same time, but rather two extremes along a single line with varying grades along the way. A sort of measurement scale.

The clerk entering the room startled Amanda and reminded her that her watch had beeped and she herself needed to get back to work.

But she was here and she needed information. Having time and not having time. Needing information and getting informed. Definitely two intersecting lines along two paths she currently needed to find an equilibrium between. Knowing she needed to find the delicate balance between, she considered her question as carefully as she could. "What is this and do you know where it is now?" Amanda asked, pointing at the star in the picture.

"You are talking about the Star of Narwist."

"Narwist?"

"People said the original owner was a wizard. Or an old coot, depending on who you asked. He apparently had a lot of followers who believed in his magic. They said he could tell the future and that he helped people crossover to the other side when they died. It's because of that belief that it hung outside of the crematorium, to help the souls of those that died from the plague cross to their afterlife."

"So was there any truth to his powers?"

The employee shook her head. "The truth is no one really knows what he was. His daughter had the rock of Narwist embedded within this star. She said that her father had always claimed that everyone came from the stars and that everyone would return to the stars. But it is said that when the plague ended there was looting and someone broke the iron and stole the rock."

"Why would they want just the rock?"

"Because it had belonged to the wizard. One of his followers probably wanted a keepsake."

Amanda thought on that for a moment. "And so this rock of Narwist hasn't been seen since?"

"No."

"I don't suppose you have a better picture of just the rock?"

"I don't know. I'd need to research it in our catalog or look in the master index to find out." The employee smiled. "That could take a little bit of time."

Amanda picked up her purse and keys. "If you can do that for me, I will be most grateful. I've got to get back to work right now. Can I give you a call later to see if you found anything?"

"Sure. Just give me a call. Let me get you a card."

Amanda followed the employee out to the main counter and took the card that the clerk offered. She stuck it in the front right pocket of her slacks. This way, she'd remember when she got to work. After thanking the employee, Amanda ran out to her car, got in, and drove back to work as quickly she could. Fortunately, as far as she could tell, no one had come in while she'd been gone and Terry wasn't standing in her office waiting for her. That meant Terry was probably sitting in his office taking a nap.

Amanda pulled out the box she'd stashed in her drawer which contained several items that had belonged to her grandmother: a cat tarot deck, the numerology reference book, the genie lamp necklace, and a key to a safety deposit box. All these items, along with the crystal ball which sat on the desk, had been left to Amanda in her grandmother's will. Amanda didn't know why of all of her grandmother's belongings, these were the specific ones left to her. Of course, she had needed the crystal ball for helping her black winged angel and she'd read enough of the numerology book to have a basic understanding. The other items were still a mystery to her. Amanda dropped the magic lamp charm back in the box: it didn't work. The cat tarot deck was cute, but Amanda didn't have the preference for cats which her grandmother did. "Cats are guardians of the dead," her grandmother had once said. "Respect their haughty nature. They need it to keep the spirits in line." So maybe it was time to follow where the key led.

The bank had once told her that the fees on the box had been prepaid for ninety years. She figured that it contained her grandmother's important papers, but she'd never gone to check. She'd only taken her mother's word for it. Now, as she twisted the key around in her fingers, she had a feeling that she should find some time to check it out. Why would her grandmother leave her these "precious" mystical items and her tax returns? That didn't seem to make sense.

She knocked on Terry's door, then stepped into his office. He sat with his feet kicked up on his desk reading a travel magazine, which he looked up over the top of as she entered.

"Can I leave half an hour early today?" she asked.

He partially closed the magazine as he looked at his watch. "You were back fifteen minutes late from lunch."

Embarrassment hit her cheeks, leaving her with a flushed and slapped feeling. "I know. I'm sorry. I'll take a full hour of personal time for it and leaving early." She hoped that concession would end his pretentious disapproval. She wasn't in the position to mention that his usual hour for lunch usually took closer to an hour and half.

He shook the magazine as he opened it again. His mouth tightened. "I suppose, unless it gets busy. Have you given me back your goal worksheet?"

He knew dang well that she hadn't. "I'll finish it this afternoon," she promised. Now, as long as no one came in this afternoon, she'd be good to leave for the bank early. If one person came through the door though, Terry might say that it was too busy for her to leave, even if that person left an hour before she was to get off work.

Terry grunted to dismiss her.

Amanda sat back down at her desk. Right before she was settled, the phone rang. She hoped this wasn't an indication of how the afternoon would go.

After taking an order to place a flight for a regular customer traveling overseas and completing the request, she pulled the goal worksheet out of her drawer.

Amanda held her pen above the paper. *What do I write?* She felt like she was in school again, trapped by a due assignment. She carefully erased her previous statement about saving the world, knowing that Terry would never understand that goal; why did one work at a travel agency when their intention was to save the world. How did one even set out to save the world? Did it even need rescuing? Maybe she would do well to clarify her own thinking too.

What are my personal development goals for the coming year, it asked, followed by a list of three numbers. Personal development? Become the best oracle I can, she thought to herself. Now that she had quit refusing her own power, she had to start to use it. Okay, maybe this assignment wasn't totally dumb. To become a better oracle, she would need to get some more tarot decks so she could read cards like her grandmother had taught her. She would need to practice with the crystal ball until the images within it became clearer. She would need to learn how to cast bones and read them. The last startled her. She had no clue where that had come from. Honestly, she wasn't even sure casting bones was a thing, or how to learn it. Who would teach such a morbid skill?

But those were her next steps. She felt that. Of course, she couldn't write those down for Terry.

She found herself reaching for the cat tarot deck and shuffling the cards. "How do I answer this question for Terry?" she whispered to the deck. King of Cups came out. Authority, control of her emotions. She already knew how one could be teased for showing otherworldly powers. She would need to control her emotions under adversity and that was another skill she'd have to acquire. Okay, personal development.

I will increase my skills, she wrote down. She didn't need to write down which skills she would increase, only that it was her goal. That was the hidden side of her goals. *Hidden Side,* she thought as she smiled to herself. A double meaning hidden in her answers. Her own personal secret. She liked it.

I will be a leader. I would like to be given my own office someday.

She wasn't sure why she wrote the last sentence, but she left it. She even wondered if it would make Terry a little nervous. It wasn't entirely false; she might like to have her own business one day. Did oracles have offices where they could advise people? She didn't see why not. As she reflected on this, she realized she'd like to do the second item as well.

So there were two answers to this question and they were big ones. Maybe the enormity of the goals would be enough to appease Terry.

Next question: *List three goals you'd like to accomplish next year.* Again there was an empty space lead by three numbers.

Make more money topped her list. An oracle making money at it. It made her laugh. Certainly she wasn't the first to think about it, but had any others ever accomplished it? She realized her knowledge of other oracles was sorely lacking.

By the number one, she put down: *Meet more people.* Oracles specifically, she thought, knowing this to be her Hidden Side.

Picking up the deck again, she shuffled while focusing on how she should answer. Six of Wands. She had to travel beyond her own boundaries and explore new horizons. She also needed the momentum for change.

Already she could see how this influenced her answers for her Hidden Side. There she was working at a travel agency and being told to move away from the known shore. She'd seen enough people signing up for adventurous travels that terrified them. Something about going somewhere new had the power to make someone excited and anxious at the same time.

That didn't tell her how to answer her question exactly. Or maybe it did, in a way. She did want to see more of the world. Here she sat making arrangements for other people, but never for herself. She kept telling herself that she couldn't take the time off now, but that someday she would take three months off to do a castle tour by bicycle. Or a cruise to see the pyramids.

But as an oracle, she should educate herself in the practices of the ancients who came before her. She needed to travel more. She put that down as number two.

Now she sat staring at the paper. How come she could only get two answers for the questions? The numbers just didn't work out. Would Terry accept these answers or would he know she was being duplicitous?

Two's. Why was the number two playing so heavily in her life right now? What was it trying to tell her?

Terry came out of his office. Between the squeak of his chair and the click of his shoes on the fake wood flooring, she'd had just enough warning to drop the cat tarot into her drawer and close it.

"Why don't you head on out?" he said. "It's been slow this afternoon.

Amanda felt relief hit her. "I will. Thank you. Tomorrow will probably be busy," she said, with an edge of hope touching her voice. "With the upcoming weekend," she added.

"You doing anything fun this weekend?" he asked.

She prayed he wasn't going to stand here and talk to her for half an hour. She reached into her drawer for her purse, hoping it would give him enough of a clue that she really was leaving. "Nope," she answered, trying to sound as flat, boring, and noncommittal as she could.

"My wife and I are going to take a drive up the coast," he said.

"That's nice." She fished her keys out of her purse. "It should be good weather for that."

Nothing quite killed a conversation like talking about the weather. Terry shifted his weight between his feet, then aimed himself back toward his office. "Well, you have a good night."

"You too," Amanda said. She watched him walk back into his office, then grabbed the tarot cards out and packaged it back into its little box before slipping it into her purse. She practically ran from the building before Terry could call her back.

At the bank, she had to sign for the safety deposit box. She remembered once signing the card at the bank, but she'd never actually been in the vault with all the boxes before. A tall blond led the way with a large ring of keys.

"What was the box number again?" the blond teller asked.

"One-twenty-eight," Amanda answered. She added the numbers, one-two-eight, together in her head: eleven, which when added again were two. That had been the same sum of five-four-zero-two: eleven, then two.

The woman stuck her key in first, then held her hand out for Amanda's key, which she inserted, then turned the two keys together. She opened the small door, then pulled her key from the lock, leaving Amanda's in the door.

"There you go," the blond said. "When you're done, close the door and take your key out. You can just exit the room back to the lobby."

"Thank you." Amanda waited until the blond teller had left the room before pulling the plastic box out of the slot. She took it to a small table with a partition dividing the area into two spaces the size of voting booths. Ignoring the feeling of claustrophobia, she pulled opened the flimsy lid off. The safety deposit box felt no more sturdy than a plastic food storage container, but Amanda guessed that if someone broke in passed the metal walls of the vault, they pretty much had access to the safety deposit boxes regardless of how the contents were stored.

She lifted the lid.

Her mother was right. A pile of papers, mostly tax returns dating back thirty years. Since grandmother was dead now, these could be destroyed. They surely didn't need to be kept for another ninety years, right?

Amanda hauled the papers out of the box, feeling a certain amount of disappointment at having to be the one to dispose of these. She briefly wondered if she could get a refund on the safety deposit box fees if she closed out the box today. It might be enough to make a good start as a nest egg for her traveling fund.

A thud came from the back of the box as something fell from between the papers. Amanda set the stack aside and reached deeper inside. She found a small box at the back. As soon as her fingers closed around the cool wood, she knew what it was and her heart skipped a beat or two.

The puzzle box had fit so differently in her hand when she was younger. Now, instead of it being too large for her, it fit comfortably in her palm, much like it had fit in her grandmother's when Amanda had seen her carrying it around the house.

Her fingertips pressed into the indentations

of the wood which she knew were little etched carvings on the box. She pulled out the not-quite-square heirloom and stared at it in amazement. It wasn't quite like she remembered. The cuts on the side definitely made it more of a rounded star. A star like the one in the picture which had been made of wrought iron.

Chills swept up her arm and Amanda turned to look around her as if expecting to see someone there. No one stood beside her.

But she was certain that she felt someone.

Amanda focused on the box. She first twisted the lid. It had to be moved to just the right spot to activate the mechanisms on the other sections of the box. Only then would they line up and spin. Her fingers twisted the pieces in the order her grandmother had taught her. Back then, it had been a game. Now it felt more like tightrope walking for her very life.

Every time she'd opened it when she was younger, her grandmother had placed a slip of paper inside which indicated Amanda's reward for opening the box. Amanda couldn't help but to wonder what was inside now. She certainly hoped it wasn't her grandmother's chocolate chip cookie recipe with a note telling her to go make some herself now.

Amanda swore she heard a chuckle beside her. Once again, Amanda looked over her shoulder. No one else was in the vault with her.

What if the bank was robbed while she was in here? What if she got shut in? She tried not to think about it. But she just couldn't shake the feeling that either she wasn't alone or that something bad was going to happen.

The final mechanism on the box slid into place and the spring clicked the lid open. Inside the cutout in the wood rested a key wrapped in a small slip of paper. Amanda took the key out and uncurled the paper from around the metal.

5402 Starlight Avenue – arcane was the note written on the paper.

The last thing she needed was a wild goose chase. Why couldn't something just be written plainly without all the covert moves? Something like: this key goes to the treasure of the oracles where you'll find the Stone of Narwist, would be nice. But no, instead, a partial address and a word. It didn't even say for certain that Starlight Avenue was here. It could be three states over in Brookville for all she knew. Or, with the word arcane, it could mean the address was from a city in the ancient world.

As her thoughts returned from her quick list of possibilities, she remembered that she'd said she would call the girl at the museum to see what information had been found.

Amanda stuck the box with the key and paper inside it into her purse. She slid the safety deposit box with its worthless tax documents back into its slot and clicked the door closed, taking out her key from the lock. She felt something move beside her, but when she looked, she was still alone.

"Done already," the blond teller asked Amanda as she left.

Amanda looked back to the vault. The presence has followed her out. "Um, yeah," she answered, unsure if she really was done. Did people normally take longer than that? Was she arousing suspicion? Was there something else she should have done? Was this feeling of being followed making her paranoid?

"You have a nice day," the teller said with a wave.

Amanda practically ran the rest of the way out of the bank. She got in her car and locked the door. It didn't help. Whatever had been in the bank vault with her was not in the car. She looked around, and as much as she didn't want to for fear that she'd see a ghastly face looking back at her, she even checked her back seat in the rear view mirror. She couldn't shake the chills.

"You saw too many horror movies as a kid," she berated herself. Once she was certain that there was no one in the car with her, she started the engine and drove out of the bank's parking lot.

But where was she going?

Starlight Avenue. She knew the answer before she even pulled out onto the street.

Amanda drove, purely letting instinct take over. She found herself in the downtown district and as she made a left turn onto a little road, she saw that the street sign read: Starlight Avenue.

Modern businesses had taken over the old warehouse district. Brick had been installed as the sidewalk here as if trying to fancy up the look of the old buildings. Retro, she was certain they would be called. Ivy grew up over the facades of most of the warehouses. One in particular was nearly covered except for the old metal door. She pulled over and sat where she could look at it from across the street. 5402, the dull metal numbers read on the door.

Amanda took out her cell phone and dialed the museum. "Hi, um, I was in there earlier taking to one of the ladies about an old photograph. I didn't get her name."

The girl responded in a chipper tone. "Oh, yeah. I think you were talking with Berri. She's been digging through the archive all afternoon. Let me get her for you."

Amanda heard the phone get set down on the counter and some muffled voices in the background. A moment later, there was a rustling sound as the phone was picked up again. "Remind me to show you how to put someone on hold," a voice said. Then Amada heard, "Hello, this is Berri."

"Hi, Berri. I was in there earlier today."

"Yeah. You asked me about the photograph

of the rock," Berri said. Her voice dropped to a whisper. "Look, I don't think you want to find the rock."

"Why not?"

There was more shuffling and possibly the sound of a door closing as if Berri was moving off into another room and shutting a door as quietly as she could. "I can't say much. I found the picture, but then these three people came in and took the picture."

"Took it?" Amanda asked. "Who were these people?"

"I don't know." Berri's voice was even softer.

"Are they still there?"

"Yes. They are going through everything."

Amanda's heart quickened. If her black-winged angel and homeless man had found the child they were seeking, it was possible there were three of them now. "What do they look like?"

"Don't laugh," Berri said quickly. "Ninjas. They look like ninjas."

"Ninjas? As in all in black with black masks?"

"Yeah."

"Do you need me to get help?" Amanda offered. "I could call the police."

"I don't think they want to hurt us, but they are taking everything having to do with the Stone of Narwist. Whatever you're doing, whatever business you're in, I think you should get out now. Forget about the rock. They obviously mean business."

The phone disconnected and Amanda heard the buzz of the simulated dial tone in her ear.

"Ninjas?" she whispered. Was that why she felt as if someone was with her? Did she have a ninja stalking her?

Amanda pulled the box from her purse and slid the purse under the passenger seat. If she were about to encounter ninjas, she didn't want them to be able to identify her.

Amanda looked at the old warehouse, studying it closely now. The old building had no windows, or at least none that she could see through the ivy.

She got out of her car and quietly tried to close the door. She lingered with her hand on her car for several moments. In her childhood, she'd played a game where she and her friends had a base and as long as they were touching their base, nothing could harm them. They were safe. She felt as if her car was now The Base. Once she removed her hand from it, she was fair game for whatever was coming. Oh, and she knew it was coming. She didn't know why, but she could still feel something following her. With a deep breath, Amanda pulled her hand off the car. Nothing happened. She wasn't attacked and nothing reared out of nothingness at her.

She began to cross the street. Fear picked up

a faster tune in her heart as she neared the building. She tried to calm herself, but it didn't work. Maybe, if she were lucky, anyone in the building would've gone home for the day.

Because people who worked in big creepy warehouses lived on a 9-to-5 schedule. That made just about as much sense as her car being a base. She glanced back over her shoulder wondering how long it would take her to get back. If she just touched her car, she would be safe once more, right?

The little voice in her head laughed at her.

What if there were just ordinary people inside? What if they had no clue what she was talking about? Would they just call an insane asylum to come and have her toted away? If that was the best response she could hope for, she'd take that. She could then put down on her goal worksheet, "to stay out of the insane asylum." Terry would laugh at that goal.

Firming her resolve, Amanda stepped up to the door and knocked. After a moment, a little panel at eye level in the door slid open with a thunk as it came to an abrupt stop within its slot. "Yes?" the person on the other side of the door asked.

Amanda really hadn't thought this through. What was she supposed to do? "Um," was all she could get out.

The brown eyeballs rolled at her. "Password?"

Oh yes. Amanda licked her lips in order to separate them so she could speak. "Arcane."

Now the eyes narrowed in suspicion. "Arcane?" For a moment, the eyes looked away as if the person glanced back over a shoulder. Amanda thought she saw brown hair beneath the black hood. The brown eyes returned. "Who sent you? Who is your sponsor?"

"Sponsor? No one sent me."

"Then how did you find out about this place?"

"My grandmother, she left me a puzzle box. It had this address in it." Amanda now realized she also a key in the box. Maybe she should've just opened the door?

"Who is your grandmother?"

"Harriet Mason," Amanda said.

"Harriet Mason?" The eyes seemed thoughtful. "Just a moment." The hatch slid closed with as much of a bang as the wood could possibly muster.

Amanda waited. She wasn't dead yet. But maybe the person had gone to get their weapon. Amanda still thought about running back to her car. But that is not what her black winged angel or the homeless man would do. No, they would tell her to stay brave. They put her on this path for a reason. She needed to see it through. It was the only way that she would understand the vision given to her by the homeless man. She wished she knew his name and could call him something other than her homeless man. It seemed so disrespectful.

The hatch slid open again and a new set of eyes looked out at her, these ones were green. "You say there was a box? Let's see this box."

Amanda lifted up the box, keeping her fingers curled around the sides of it so that she pointed the top toward the person. The owner of the new eyeballs at the door gasped.

The box meant something.

The woman behind the panel was pushed aside as much older and wiser eyes came into view. "It's Friday the 13th and you must be Amanda Bellock. Your grandmother said you'd come to the realization on a Friday the 13th. Did you bring your grandmother with you?"

A mixture of shock and sadness went through Amanda. "I would've thought that you knew. My grandmother passed away several years ago."

The corners of these older eyes wrinkled and picked up a certain twinkle. "And that doesn't answer my question. Did you bring your grandmother with you?"

Amanda stepped backwards away from the door. "No."

The hatch slid closed. So it would seem that a sponsor had to be there with their inductee to get into the special group, Amanda thought. What was she to do now?

Before she turned away she heard the door

slide open. The metal door didn't open like a normal door, but rather slid along rails to the side. An elderly woman whose perfectly coiffed hair had hundreds of little, soft, silver curls stood in the doorway. She was just shorter than Amanda and came out in her white blouse and blue jeans extending a hand toward Amanda.

Amanda took her hand but the woman didn't want to shake it but rather patted the back of Amanda's hand. "So your grandmother could never teach you anything? Yet now you find yourself ready?" The woman turned still holding onto Amanda's hand and led her into the building.

The warehouse smelled like the forest with a bit of sage and other herbs. She saw several bundles of herbs hanging upside down above what looked like a thick wooden table that had once been used to carve meat. Along the walls there were rows of tall bookshelves completely packed with books. Wherever there wasn't a bookshelf, there was a filing or curio cabinets. There were three doorways out of this initial room. Amanda couldn't see what was in the other rooms very well as the doors were closed or left slightly ajar allowing a view through a gap of an inch or two. Soft instrumental music played overhead.

Off to the left, five chairs circled around a wooden coffee table in a cozy sitting area. They stepped up on the thick rug which covered the area and Amanda felt the deep plush slide under her feet. She had a memory of taking off her shoes before stepping onto a rug at her grandmother's when she entered one of the auxiliary rooms.

"Matrice, are you sure are it is okay to be talking to her? To be exposing our secrets?" One of the original faces from the door said. Both women who had looked out the slight panel at her now stood just a few feet away from her. They both were wearing black robes with hoods that lightly covered their hair. "We don't know anything about her, like if she's even telling the truth."

"We have yet to begin to discuss anything, secret or otherwise." The older woman looked at the younger women with a slight smile, the kind you would give a child who was telling you an interesting but thoroughly incorrect story. "She comes to us with the puzzle box and the password. If her story is not the truth, it will be found out soon enough."

"Yes, Matrice," the woman said with a nod of her head.

The older woman called Matrice guided Amanda and motioned for her to have a seat in one of the padded chairs. Amanda did as requested, but sat on the edge uneasily as if the elegance of the chair was overwhelming to her. In truth, everything about the inside of this building was overwhelming to her. Matrice took a look at Amanda, giving a stern nod of her head, before she sat down on the other side of a little wooden coffee table in a chair that matched the one that Amanda now sat in. Matrice leaned back laying her arms out elegantly over the arms of the chair as she politely crossed one knee over the other. The woman held such a dignified look to her even as she sat there in this little chair that Amanda felt a certain respect for her instantly. "So you're grandmother's name was Harriet Mason, is that correct?"

Amanda barely managed to nod.

"And what is your name child?"

"Amanda Bellock."

"And what of your mother? What is her name?"

"Beverly Mason Bellock," Amanda announced slowly and carefully. It felt very odd using her mother's maiden name.

Matrice shook her head. "I don't remember a Beverly Bellock. Did she practice the old ways?"

Amanda curtailed her cough. "My mother wasn't a believer in anything that my grandmother did." Amanda wanted to add that she hadn't been a believer either until recently. The words sat there on the tip of her tongue but would not come off. If they knew the truth, they might just send her out the door now before she had a chance to figure out what this fascinating place was. The more she sat here, the more she looked around, the more fascinated she became with place. It had magic. Real magic. The exact thing that her grandmother used to tell her about. The exact thing that she had felt when the homeless man had touched her hand.

"And you probably laughed right along with your mother, believing that your grandmother was a kook, didn't you?"

Matrice knew. Amanda could not hide it from her. The truth was out of the bag. Or in a fashion. "I didn't want anything to do with it because I wanted to be popular with kids my age."

Matrice gave a little knowing smile. "Do not fear. We all understand how wisdom comes along with a certain lack of caring about what others think about us. That is what happens to everyone in time. And the more we learn to be ourselves and not care what others believe about us or think about us, brings us closer to understanding a greater truth."

Amanda didn't know what this greater truth was that Matrice spoke about, though she had a feeling. The same kind of feeling that she'd had when confronted by the black-winged angel and the homeless man.

The two women in black robes return shortly each carrying a tray which they set down on the coffee table. One tray had a little teapot and some dainty looking teacups along with a small assortment of cookies. The other tray had a larger decanter and mugs along the sugar and cream and some sticks of biscotti.

Matrice uncurled her legs and leaned forward. "May I offer you some tea or coffee?" She said

Amanda hesitated for a moment, the little voice of fear screaming that they could've easily poisoned anything here. She tried to be rational. Why would they do that to her? Her rational thoughts were not winning out. It took a lot of strength for her to remain seated in the chair and not go running for the door. "Tea is fine." She preferred coffee if she were going to have a choice between the two. For some reason, tea seemed more fitting for this situation.

Matrice flipped two of the teacups over and began pouring from the teapot. "I do hope you like black tea. I've never quite acquired a taste for the green teas." Having filled both cups, she set the teapot down then dropped two sugar cubes into her tea using little finger-sized silver tongs. She raised the sugar cubes toward Amanda, with the tongs poised above them.

"Yes please," Amanda said. She watched Matrice drop two sugar cubes into her teacup.

Matrice waved her elegantly long fingers toward the tray of coffee. "We do have cream if you would like some in your tea as well," Matrice offered.

"No, thank you."

Matrice picked up a spoon, tiny and silver, almost like one used to feed a child with, and began to stir the tea within each cup. Then she handed a cup to Amanda. Taking her own cup into her hands, she sat back and crossed her legs once more. "You do not feel a thing, do you child?"

"I don't understand what you mean." Amanda blew across the top of the hot tea and then took a cautious sip.

Matrice lifted a hand away from her cup and turned it in the air, an easy fluid motion that made Amanda wonder how this woman could move all the time with such grace. It didn't seem possible. Even her black-winged angel hadn't moved so easily. "You have indeed brought your grandmother with you, but you are not aware of it. She stands right behind you now with her hand on your shoulder, but you do not feel it."

Amanda jumped at those words, nearly spilling her tea all over her lap. She looked over each shoulder trying to see this vision of her grandmother, but she could not. "I don't understand how you see this. There's no one there."

"Your grandmother said she had a hard time explaining to you what she did, that you had no comprehension and generally no memory of the conversation after you'd had it." Matrice looked toward one of the young girls wearing the black robes. "Please bring some geranium and some orange. We'll be needing the memory enhancement."

The girl nodded as she spun on her foot and rushed into another room.

"You mean, she told me but I don't remember it?" Amanda asked.

"That would appear to be the case," Matrice said. "So, it might be that she taught you more than you remember. Just because you chose to suppress the memories does not mean that you do not have them."

The woman returned with quick, shuffling steps and bowed as she set a smaller tray containing several items down beside the refreshment trays. "Here you are, Grand Mother."

Matrice leaned forward to pick up a couple of amber colored vials. She rose and stepped closer to Amanda. "Have you ever used essential oils before?"

"No," Amanda replied. "But I've heard about them." She wanted to be quick with some knowledge, still feeling unsettled with the belief that they might throw her out at any moment.

"There is no great magic about them," Matrice said, again smiling. "Just distilled oils. I'd like to put them on you. It should make you relax and open up your thoughts. If you have sensitive skin, we can dilute them in coconut oil."

"I'm fine," Amanda said hastily. As far as she'd known, she'd rarely had an allergy to anything in her life. Her grandmother had always commented that the family had come from hardy stock, whatever that meant.

"Lean back and tip your head for me."

Amanda rested back in the chair and looked at the ceiling to stretch her neck. She felt a couple drops of oil land on her skin, then Matrice's cool fingers were there rubbing the moisture along Amanda's throat.

"There," Matrice said. "Now just breathe and relax."

Amanda inhaled deeply of the oils on her skin. It wasn't hard to do since they smelled pretty good. She found herself naturally relaxing and finally settled down into the chair where she sat. Matrice looked pleased and Amanda returned her smile.

"Just rest now, my dear," Matrice said. "Don't try to force anything. Let it come naturally."

As Amanda let all the tension just exhale right out of her chest, she wanted to close her eyes but she didn't dare. These were still strangers surrounding her and she wasn't quite ready to let her guard down around them. Especially ones that wore black robes.

Matrice seemed to sense her discomfort and waved a hand toward the girls. They quickly turned and left the room. It seemed they couldn't scamper away fast enough either. It made Amanda wonder what had them so scared.

"Maybe I should tell you a little bit about our

order," Matrice said as she settled back in her own chair. "Every world has secret societies. It seems to be a natural inclination for people to want to huddle together and be part of a group that no one else knows about. Some groups practice doing no harm, while others hide together in secrecy while plotting to destroy the world. It has been that way since the beginning of the Onesong and it will probably continue to be that way until the end, should there ever be an end."

"What is this Onesong?" Amanda asked

"In its simplest terms, the Onesong is the energy that runs through everything. Everything you see and everything you don't see is made up of energy. That energy comes from the Onesong."

As Matrice spoke, Amanda knew the truth of it all. She could feel it moving through her, stirring, awakening. Yes, she did have knowledge of this Onesong and exactly what it was but on a level that she did not have words for. It was a feeling rather than something even like an abstract construct. It was just there. It always had been, and it always would be. It felt like something she could depend on. In the same way that she knew that the sun would rise each day. Of course, as she now understood, the Onesong was responsible for the rising of that sun and would continue to be for many years to come.

Matrice nodded, seeming to know that Amanda understood. She continued, "We are a secret society here. We are soul collectors, collectors and guardians of energy that would otherwise be forgotten. The wizard who held the Stone of Narwist came, retired actually, to this planet during the time of the plague. If the history is true, too many people were put into the crematoriums before their time had really come. That makes for terribly chaotic energies. Anytime there is a plague or war or disaster which takes too many people all at once, there comes a time for the soulcolist to move into action and collect the souls of the dead."

"So that is what you do here? Collect souls?"

With the ever-present grace that Amanda was beginning to recognize with Matrice, the woman gave a small, perfect, polite shake of her head. "Not for some time. We are patiently waiting for that time when we have a soulcolist back in our midst. I fear our wait must endure even longer."

Amanda felt relief loosen the knot in her chest. Until now, she didn't realize how much tension had built up there. She didn't want to be someone who collected souls. After all, weren't they just supposed to cross over on their own? What happened to these gathered souls? She wasn't certain she was ready for the answer right now. "So, what do you do? My grandmother spoke of a prophecy."

"Good, you remember that. What else do you remember?"

With her eyelids feeling heavy, Amanda relaxed back into the chair. She closed her eyes for just a moment. The memory of the homeless man returned with clarity. He had touched her hand, his rough, weathered skin pressing against hers. He had given her a vision. As if she were rolling back the moment, she saw it in reverse, then forward again as if in slow motion. He had touched her hand, energy had come into her. There was more. Miniscule cuts in his fingers had snagged into her skin, injecting her with his own essence and pouring forth something into her that she could never have come upon by herself.

"What did you just experience, child?"

Amanda opened her eyes to see Matrice leaning forward in her chair. "Nothing," Amanda said ruefully. "But something happened to me recently and I know there's more to it, but I can't quite figure out how to access it."

"Relax," Matrice said. "Nothing comes when you push it. There is a fine nature in being calm and patient."

Amanda understood that calm and patient were good descriptions for Matrice's elegant grace. Nothing was hurried. She had found the center point of the fine nature of which she spoke. Of course, that was easy for Matrice to say, but Amanda knew that once she had accessed this secret, her life would change. How was she supposed to patiently sit back and wait for that to happen? Those were the kind of thoughts that allowed someone to lose years of their life to procrastination rather than moving forward with their goals and ambitions.

As if sensing her thoughts, Matrice gave a smile and said, "The perfect balance comes from blending one's temperament with action. You must always proceed forward knowing your intentions, but release the expectations of how it comes to you. Too many people fall flat to one side or the other, but walking in the center will get you much further."

"How long did it take you to figure out the balance?"

"Far longer than I would have liked." Matrice's smiling countenance took on a sly look. "Let's see if we can make your transition so much faster as you follow in my wisdom."

Amanda liked the way Matrice phrased the offer. It helped her feel as if she didn't have to do it all alone. "How can we do that?"

"You have found your way here and that alone is a big accomplishment. Be very proud of yourself and know that you have accomplished more than others in your position." Matrice paused. "Do sit back and try to return to that prior moment where you were. Let's start there."

Amanda closed her eyes and once again

thought about her visit from the black-winged angel and the homeless man. He had touched her hand. The rough skin of his fingers caught on hers. She had felt something. Energy. Something more. A memory. No!

Her future.

She stood on top of a building all dressed in black. Not the black robes these women wore, but outwardly normal clothes, except for the caplet around her shoulders and the mask currently lifted above her eyebrows. She reached up and pulled it down as her brown hair tussled in the wind. She turned as if looking at someone and smiled. "Let's go," the vision of herself said happily.

A couple of people also dressed in form-fitting outwear ran by her, jumping fearlessly off the roof. Amanda followed and as she felt herself falling, she spread her arms out. Material extended out from her arms to her torso and caught the updraft of air. Suddenly she was flying like her black-winged angel. A moment later, she was following the others as she unclipped the material from her arms and went into a building. They had made it stealthily inside.

Before the vision faded from her, Amanda noticed that the sky was a different color and realized she was on another world. Never, not once, had she ever seen a yellow sky on her world. She didn't realize it could be anything other than the soft lavender she knew so well.

As Amanda opened her eyes, she involuntarily whispered the one word that rolled around in her mind, "Ninjas." That's what the girl at the museum had said, that ninjas had come inside and were looking for the same information she had been.

"You're not oracles," Amanda said. "You're ninjas!"

Matrice remained seated, still giving a smile, though it didn't feel as genuine as it had a moment before. No, this was much more practiced, tolerant even. "No, we are soulcolists and we guard the Stone of Narwist now."

"I was following the path of the Stone through history and asked the girl at the museum about it. She was going to look it up for me," Amanda said. "But someone came in and collected all the pictures from their archives. I was told that the people who raided the museum looked like ninjas."

That actually brought the smile off of Matrice's face. She sat there, completely motionless and just staring at Amanda for a few seconds before she uncurled her legs and rose from her chair. "Char, Beth, we have trouble," she said, nearly tripping over her feet as she hurried off the rugged area.

The two women in the black robes came rushing into the room. "Trouble?"

"Masters have come."

Char and Beth stopped in their tracks now. The three women all seemed to be paused in time as Amanda wondered what had gotten so deeply into Matrice that she was no longer graceful.

"Are you sure?" one of the women asked.

"Then it really is time," said the other.

Amanda suddenly found three pairs of eyes staring at her. "Get the stone," Matrice stated quickly.

The women went running off.

Matrice turned back toward Amanda.

Setting her teacup down on the table, Amanda used the momentum to get up on her feet. "It's been a long day. I just got off work. I'm tired and hungry. I really should be going now."

Matrice didn't look pleased at Amanda's many excuses. "Sit back down."

Amanda dropped back to her chair.

Matrice came and stood over Amanda. She stared down like a vulture in a tree watching its prey. Gone was the soft and graceful woman. She'd become stern and dark. Amanda knew that if she made it out of here tonight, she would never use the cat tarot or crystal ball again. She'd been correct in leaving that life, this odd life, behind.

"I should have known," Matrice hissed. "A Mason always courts trouble."

Amanda wanted to slink out of the chair. "I'm s-sorry," she said. "I don't know what you're talking about." She leaned away from Matrice.

"I thought you were here to help us."

"I'm here because I'm curious. I still don't know what's going on." Amanda spun around as she fled the chair. She knew she'd have to step backwards, but she didn't want to take her eyes off of Matrice.

Matrice snarled. She advanced on Amanda like a stalking panther. Amanda backed up the same number of steps, knowing she drew closer to the brick wall than she would have liked.

"It's Friday the thirteenth and a Mason is here." Matrice sounded as if all this should make perfect sense to Amanda. It didn't. She felt like it should add up, but she couldn't calculate any sense out of it.

"I'll go. It's been a nice visit, but I really must be going," Amanda said as she tried to sidle down along the length of the wall.

"What have you taken?"

Now they thought she was a thief? "Nothing!" Amanda shouted back.

"You brought an energy in here with you. Who was it?"

"You said it was my grandmother. I don't know that I brought anything in here with me." Rage clouded over her. "That was a really cruel thing of you to say, you know? I miss my grandmother."

The two women in the black robes came

running out. One held a stone the size of someone's clenched fist her in palm.

Amanda smiled.

"No, you don't!" Matrice cried out. She turned toward the women, but only made it partially around before a person dressed in black materialized from the shadow Amanda cast on the brick wall.

"Mason, collect your belonging," the newcomer said.

"Run, girls, run," Matrice shouted. "The Masters are here!"

Two more ninjas stepped from dark shadows, stopping Char and Beth before they could flee.

Amanda felt energy gathering all around and saw one of the doorways alter slightly to the left. Char disappeared through the door, which shifted back to the wall. Beth reached out for the ninja.

"No!" Matrice screamed all too late. As Beth touched the ninja, she imploded to a pile of dust. "This is all your fault," Matrice yelled at Amanda.

"You said it yourself: Masons court trouble." Amanda wasn't certain why the words came out of her mouth. It felt like she was awakening from a long dream. She pivoted on her foot, letting her other foot gently swing out as she spun. She felt a brief lift of air which tousled the ends of her hair. At halfway around, she realized she was on the upper floor of the building with no idea of how she'd gotten here, except that she knew she was and she'd done it on purpose. She continued to spin and came nearly face to face with Char. "Give me the Stone," Amanda said, reaching her hand out.

"I can't believe you would betray us," Char said, tears in her eyes.

Matrice had said nearly the same words, but Char looked genuinely hurt.

"I don't even know you," Amanda countered.

"Yes, you do," Char said. She reached up with her free hand to lower her hood. "Why don't you remember?"

Amanda felt like she should know the face that looked back at her, like an old memory just out of reach. It made her world feel distorted and strange.

"You can't touch the Stone," Char warned.

Amanda reached out and took the Stone.

It took her to her knees. She barely managed to hold onto the Stone of Narwist as she crumpled to the floor.

"You weren't supposed touch the Stone," Char cried out. "Give it back. I won't tell the Grand Mother that you held it. I promise. Just give it back to me."

Amanda looked down at the stone in her hands. It didn't look too different than a crystal, though certainly not clear like the crystal ball she'd had on her desk. It had several facets to it and fracture lines that ran through the stone itself, giving it many cloudy veils. In each section partitioned by the white curtain, she could see images, many of them related to the plague and the undead victims burned while still trying to survive. So many souls. So much energy. So much needless waste and chaos. She felt like she might drown in it all if she didn't hand the Stone back.

She couldn't.

Matrice appeared and hesitated in the doorway for a moment before rushing over to Amanda and collapsing down beside her. "Do you remember now?"

Amanda glanced away from the Stone to Matrice. "I do. I remember it all."

The stories her grandmother use to tell, the visits from the Masters who hid skills away in Amanda's head, the prophecy that the Stone of Narwist would return to the stars in the hands of the newest Master, training with the young soulcolists, becoming an outcast while wanting to be part of a group. Oh, to belong to something instead of being shunned... Amanda's longings had generated an idea: she would learn to live in the world and bring the energy back to the soulcolists. Together they would reprogram the Stone and release the soulcolists of this world from their fate.

Her grandmother had never said that she

would be the one to break the prophecy. She had known that a trick like this would never work.

Mathematics ruled the cosmos. When one tried to change the calculations, the numbers no longer added up.

But the homeless man had given her a new outlook of the fate that Amanda had once wanted to deny. The greater universe at large needed her help. The Stone had waited for her, coming to this planet so many years before in the hands of a soulcolist who collected the energy of those who had suffered through the plague and died. So many things had to work out just right for them all to get here to this point now.

The three Masters emerged from the wall behind her and two bent down to help Amanda to her feet. "Come, Mason," the third one said. "We have much energy to be collecting. You are needed throughout the universe."

Amanda looked to them, their faces covered partially over with a black cloth. All she could see was their eyes. Eyes she trusted. She now belonged.

Let the future begin.

Ready for another quest?

Sign up for Dawn Blair's newsletter to learn about new releases, get access to fun and free stuff, hear about events, and more!

It's easy.

Go to **www.morningskystudios.com/newsletter** to join the adventure.

About the Author

Dawn Blair grew up on a ranch in a rural Nevada town. The old buildings provided inspiration for her imagination and she thrived on stories of unicorns, princesses, heroic knights, and hidden doors to other dimensions.

Today, she loves creating worlds and telling stories for people to enjoy. In addition to writing, she also paints and illustrates.

Find more books by Dawn Blair at
www.morningskystudios.com

www.ingramcontent.com/pod-product-compliance
Lightning Source LLC
Chambersburg PA
CBHW020651130626
46552CB00003B/1498